I0537552

Destiny's
BIG DECISION

Look for these and other books about Linelle Destiny in the Linelle Destiny Series:

Visit www.thesecretsistersclub.com

Linelle Destiny Series

Destiny's
BIG DECISION

Dr. Alicia Holland
Illustrations by Anoop PC

No parts of this book may be used or reproduced by an means, graphic, electronic, or mechanical, including photocopying, recording, taping or by any information storage retrieval system without the written permission of the author except in the case of brief quotations embodied in critical articles and reviews.

This book may be ordered through booksellers or by contacting:

iGlobal Educational Services, LLC
13785 Highway 183, Suite 125
Austin, Texas 78750
www.iglobaleducation.com
512-761-5898

Because of the dynamic nature of the Internet, any web addresses or links contained in this book may have changed since publication and may no longer be valid. The views expressed in this work are solely those of the author and do not necessarily reflect the views of the publisher, and the publisher hereby disclaims any responsibility for them.

This is a work of fiction. Names, characters, businesses, places, events, and incidents are either the products of the author's imagination or used in a fictitious manner. Any resemblance to actual persons, living or dead, or actual events is purely coincidental.

Linelle Destiny Series: Destiny's Big Decision

Copyright © 2015 Alicia Holland, EdD. All rights reserved.

ISBN: 1944346066

ISBN-13: 978-1-944346-06-5

Acknowledgements

I want to first honor God for placing in my heart to share my story with others. It was He whom brought Karen and I together to manifest this project. I am so grateful for Karen Hendry as she took my notes and helped write this fictitious book. There are truly no words to express my gratitude as you are truly a blessing.

I also want to thank Surendra Gupta for his creativity in formatting and Anoop PC for his creativity in bringing life to the designs and illustrations in this book series. Both of you are amazing!

Dedication

I dedicate this book series to my beautiful and talented daughters, Georgia and Amaiya Johnson. Remember, you are valued, loved, and competent. You are worthy!

Part I:
Grade Nine

Chapter One
Big Dreams

Destiny walks into the crowded hallway, her locker code clutched tightly in her hand, and looks around for Barbara. She's sure Barbara will be happy to find out that she is staying in their class this year, but she hasn't told her the good news yet because Barbara just got back from her grandma's house yesterday.

Destiny sees Barbara's slim frame. She is standing with her back against her locker and Haley is hovering over her, dark curls pulled back in a clip. The way Barbara is shrinking back, it looks like she wishes she could just climb into her locker and disappear.

Destiny rolls her eyes and stalks over to them.

When she gets there, Haley's taunting voice reaches her ears. "Most of the Secret Sisters Club members are in my club now *and* we have boys as club members." Snooty can't even begin to describe Haley's tone.

Destiny laughs, causing Haley to whip her head around. "Really, Haley? Do four girls from the old club count as most of them?"

Haley turns from Barbara, who visibly relaxes now that she's not under Haley's icy stare, and focuses her attention on Destiny. "Well, well. Look who it is. Skies High School's beloved student returns," she sneers. "You know, Destiny, you never should have messed with me. You aren't going to know what hit you this year."

Destiny raises an eyebrow and then turns to Barbara. "I'm so glad to see you!" She gives Barbara a big hug. "How was your summer?"

"Well, miss know-it-all," says Haley as she flounces off in a huff, "you'll find out what's in store for you soon enough!"

Barbara heaves a sigh of relief and they start walking down the hallway. "I'm glad you showed up when you did," she says. "Thanks for getting rid of her. Did you hear what she said about her club?"

"Yeah, I heard her."

"Do you think she's telling the truth, that she has a lot of members?" Barbara asks.

"I think she's full of hot air," says Destiny. "We'll get the Secret Sisters Club back up and running and it will be better than ever. Now tell me about your summer."

"It was great! I had lots of fun swimming and biking and Grandma taught me how to knit! I am glad to be home, though. How about you? You must have been busy."

Destiny nods and Barbara goes on, "I wrote to Kendall every week, like we promised. Did you?"

Destiny flinches at that. "I did at first," she says, biting her lower lip, "but I haven't in a while. Tutoring has kept me so busy. How is she?"

"She's good. She misses us like crazy and she was really nervous about starting school today, but she likes her new house and made a new friend on her street. Miranda, I think. They'll be in the same class."

"That's good to hear," says Destiny.

"What about you?" Barbara asks. "Have you decided to skip a grade?"

Destiny's face lights up. "That's what I wanted to tell you! I've decided I don't want to skip ninth grade," she beams. "I really just want to stay with my friends."

"Yay!" shouts Barbara. "Come on in here. I want to check my hair." They duck into the bathroom.

Barbara leans into the big mirror and starts to touch up her hair. "I'm so happy you'll be staying in our class this year, Destiny, but are you sure? I mean, skipping a grade is a really big deal."

Destiny nods as they look at each other's reflections in the mirror. "I have thought about it for weeks. Believe me, I'm sure!"

"Have you told Curtis?" Barbara asks.

"I haven't seen him yet and I haven't talked to him in a few weeks." Curtis is Destiny's boyfriend, but with her being busy with tutoring and him at basketball camp most of the summer, they haven't seen much of each other.

"I'm sure he'll be *almost* as happy as I am when he finds out," says Barbara.

"Well," says Destiny, her face turning crimson, "he would be happy I am staying if he knew I had the chance to skip a grade."

"You never told him?" Barbara's eyes nearly popped out of her head. "Why on earth didn't you?"

Destiny shrugs. "I honestly don't know, Barbara. Maybe I knew deep inside I wasn't going to do it, so I didn't want to get him worried for nothing."

"Wow, I wish you had of spared me from worrying like that," says Barbara and she winks at me.

When they leave the washroom, they meet Julianna in the hallway. "Hey, Julianna," says Destiny. "How was your summer?"

"Hi, Destiny," Julianna almost shouts. "Hi, Barbara. My summer was great! Yours?"

Both Destiny and Barbara nod in unison and say, "Great!"

Julianna asks, "Are y'all gonna try out for the track team this year?"

"I plan on it," Destiny replies. Barbara shakes her head.

Julianna starts almost vibrating on the spot, she is so excited. "Oh, Destiny, that's great! The tryouts are today after school."

The three of them reach their classroom and go inside to take their seats. This is going to be a great year, thinks Destiny, as the bell rings and their teacher starts to take attendance.

Out of breath after running, Destiny stops for a drink at the water cooler. It's a hot day, not a cloud in the sky, and Destiny is sweating like crazy, but she thinks she did well. Julianna joins her and says, "You were great, Destiny! I don't know if I can keep

up or if I'll make the team. I wish I was as fast as you. Then I'd be in for sure."

"Julianna, I'm sure you'll be great," says Destiny. "You know I'll be cheering you on when you run."

"Thanks, Destiny," Julianna replies after taking a drink. "I can always count on you. You know, you have your own private cheerleader."

"Huh?"

"Curtis has been sitting in the bleachers watching you the entire time," says Julianna.

"Really?"

Julianna nods and Destiny looks around for Curtis. When she spots him in the bleachers, she smiles and waves at him. He waves back, but he seems distracted.

"I wonder what's up with him," says Destiny. "Did you see that? He waved, but he looks uncomfortable."

Julianna shrugs. "It's probably because it's so hot outside. My, but you're lucky to have a boyfriend like him. He is so supportive."

"Yeah," says Destiny, but she feels unsure.

When the tryouts are done, Coach GoLucky speaks to the group. "Great job today, all of you! I wish I had room for all of you on the team, but there are only ten spots. I'll post the results tomorrow on the bulletin board outside the gym." With that, he dismisses them.

"I can't wait until we get the results," says Julianna.

Destiny agrees, "Me, too."

"See ya, Destiny," Julianna says. "I have to run, but I'll catch up with you later."

"Okay, see you later."

Destiny decides to go see Curtis. He is no longer sitting in the bleachers, so she looks around and sees him not far away. He looks like he is waiting for someone. As Destiny starts to walk toward him, Trinity runs up and gives him a big hug.

Destiny freezes for a moment. She has never seen Curtis hug Trinity before. It seems weird, but she makes herself resume walking toward them.

"Hey Curtis," she says when she reaches them.

Curtis jumps at the sound of her voice. "Destiny! Oh, hi." He doesn't meet her eyes. "It's good to see you."

"It's good to see you, too. I missed you this summer."

"Yeah, sure. Me, too."

Curtis still won't meet Destiny's eyes, but Trinity is standing next to him with a big smirk on her face. "Hey, Destiny. Nice job at the tryouts."

"Thanks, Trinity. You, too. So, what's with the hug? You guys seem to be getting along well."

Curtis fidgets as he answers. "Oh, Trinity is just a friend."

"I've never seen you hug your friends like that before," says Destiny, getting an uneasy feeling in the pit of her stomach.

"Destiny, stop being so possessive," says Trinity. "Really! You're starting to sound just like Haley." She turns to Curtis, "Come on, Curtis. You can show me what you learned at basketball camp before I go home." And she leads him away, leaving Destiny standing there, completely confused about what just happened. Somehow, she knows it isn't good.

Chapter 2
Worries

"Destiny, can you help me with this question?" asks Julianna. "I just don't get it."

"Um, Destiny? Are you in there?" Barbara waves a hand in front of Destiny's face.

"Huh?" Destiny blinks and focuses on her friends. "Oh, sorry. Just day dreaming, I guess."

"You're not just day dreaming, Destiny," says Julianna. "You haven't been with us this whole tutoring session."

"Yeah, what's got you so distracted?" asks Barbara. "Boy trouble?"

Destiny sighs and looks at her friends. She has been feeling glum about this for days and hasn't spoken with anyone about it. "Yes, it's boy trouble. I'm not sure Curtis wants to go out with me anymore."

Barbara looks mortified. "Gee, Destiny. I was just joking about the boy trouble. I didn't know. I'm sorry."

"It's okay."

"What's the problem?" asked Julianna.

"He is spending so much time with Trinity. He says they are just friends, but I just don't get it. Why would he spend so much more time with this 'friend' than he spends with me? I've barely seen him at all since school started."

"Destiny, honey," says Barbara, "I'm sure there has to be an explanation for it."

"Like what?" asks Destiny.

"Well...," Barbara pauses, seeming uncertain about what to say. "Maybe you've been so busy he hasn't really been able to spend time with you. I know *I've* hardly seen you since school started."

Destiny looks at Julianna and Julianna nods her agreement. "I don't know," says Destiny. "It still seems weird. I get that I've been busy, but he hasn't even really tried to see me." I won't cry, Destiny thinks. I won't cry over a boy.

But Barbara and Julianna can see how upset she is. Barbara puts her arm around Destiny's shoulders and says, "Well, I'm sure there is a reasonable explanation for it. He was so into you at the start of summer vacation that. I just can't imagine he'd dump you for Trinity."

"Sure," agreed Julianna.

"Yeah, sure," said Destiny, but her gut told her something very different.

Destiny fidgets at her desk. The weeks have passed by and the Secret Sisters Club has been reformed. Destiny and the others restarted the school newspaper and have been working really hard to make the club better than ever.

Most of the girls that were members the previous year have rejoined. Some want to be members of both clubs, the Secret

Sisters Club and Haley's club, The Blue Stars. This is all right with Destiny, but Haley won't allow it. If a girl is a member of the Secret Sisters Club, then she can't be a member of The Blue Stars. For this reason, membership in the Secret Sisters Club has grown larger than that of The Blue Stars, and that has become a thorn in Haley's side.

Despite her dedication to the Secret Sisters Club and her friends, Destiny has other things to worry about. The ACT is coming up and Destiny is worried about it. This is an important test for determining whether or not a high school student will get into college when they graduate and she desperately wants to go to college.

Classes are about to start for the day and the school counselor, Mrs. Pathway, is due to come in and talk to the class about the ACT. Destiny is anxious to know what she needs to do to prepare.

Attendance is taken, and finally, Mrs. Pathway arrives. "Hello class," she says. "I'm here to talk with you about the American College Testing or ACT. This is a test that indicates your level of college readiness. Preparation is important for this test. The higher the score you receive, the better the college you can get into."

Destiny raises her hand. "Yes, Destiny," says Mrs. Pathway.

"What if we score too low? Does that mean we won't get into college? Will we have another chance to take the test?"

"This year it is more of a practice test. You will have the opportunity to take the test again next year, but Destiny, there really is nothing to worry about. Most people do fine and I'm certain you will."

"What grade do we need to make on the test to get into college?" Destiny asks.

"The grade you need to get into college depends on the college. Different colleges have different admission requirements. The average grade for the test is 21. But again, you are in the ninth grade so this is just a practice test. You don't need to worry if you don't score high enough. It will help you know what you need to work on to do better when it really counts."

But Destiny is not satisfied. "Even though this is for practice, what if you scored really high on it?" she asks.

"Anyone who scores a 34 or higher would be accepted into an early college program. Now, if there are no more questions," Mrs. Pathway says, making it clear that the question period is over, "let's talk about how to prepare for the test."

Destiny listens carefully and makes a lot of notes. She wants to get a good mark on the test so she can go to college.

Destiny spills some milk on the counter when she is pouring it into her bowl. She already had to clean up the cereal she spilled just moments before. As she is cleaning up the milk, her momma comes into the kitchen. "Now child, what are you making such a mess for?"

"Sorry, momma. Just distracted, I guess."

"What's on your mind? Is it that test you keep going on about?"

"Yes. The ACT. It's today and I want to do really well on it, Momma. I really want to go to college."

"Well, honey, I know what you want, but you need to keep your feet on the ground and your head out of the clouds. There ain't no way your Pop and I can pay for college."

Destiny feels like someone is squeezing her heart, just trying to break it into a million pieces. "But how will I ever go to college?" she says in what is nearly a whisper.

"Honey, I know how important it is to you." Momma puts a hand on Destiny's shoulder. "It's early yet and you are a smart girl. Anything can happen. Just work hard and maybe you can get a scholarship. Where there's a will, there's a way."

By the time Destiny gets on the bus, she is completely distraught. She slumps down in the seat and waits for Barbara's stop. When Barbara joins her, she can tell right away that something is wrong with Destiny.

"What's up, Destiny?"

Tears begin to well up in Destiny's eyes and she fights to keep them from spilling out. "Momma just told me that she and Pop won't be able to afford to send me to college. I don't know what I'm going to do. I have to go to college!"

Barbara looks at Destiny, a serious expression on her face. "Destiny, you are the smartest, most resourceful person I know. If anyone can find a way to get to college, it's you. Where there's a will, there's a way."

Destiny laughs a little. "That's what Momma said."

"Well, you can't argue with your Momma," says Barbara with a wink.

Destiny settles into her desk and sets out her pencil, eraser, and ruler. Despite the encouragement form Barbara, her Momma's words weigh on her mind. If they can't pay for her college education, how will she ever get one?

Oh well, Destiny thinks. I'll just focus on writing the test right now. That has to come first anyway.

She waits for the test to begin.

Chapter 3
Betrayal and Disappointment

✧ ✧ ✧

"Hey, Destiny!"

Destiny cringes as she closes her locker. Haley's voice has been grating on her nerves these past few weeks. Maybe it seems extra irritating this morning because they will be getting the results back from the ACT today and that really has Destiny's nerves on edge. In any case, Destiny still braces for the confrontation with Haley like she's bracing for an impact. Maybe she'll just go away, Destiny thinks.

No such luck.

"So, Destiny," Haley reaches Destiny as she starts to walk toward class. "Have you seen your man lately?"

"What is that supposed to mean, Haley?"

"Oh, nothing really. But maybe you should pay more attention to him. Watch what he's up to, you know? It might open your eyes. That's all."

Destiny stops walking and turns to look at Haley. "Open my eyes?"

"Yeah, you know. To reality?"

"What reality?" asks Destiny, her patience, thin to begin with, wearing to the point of snapping.

"Well," says Haley, "just that maybe you should know how he's spending his time and who he's spending it with."

"Haley," snaps Destiny, "what's happening between Curtis and me is none of your business."

"Touchy, touchy," says Haley, with a smirk on her face, yet her voice sounds so innocent when she says, "I only wanted to help. You know, give you a heads up and all."

"I don't need your help," says Destiny, walking away from Haley.

"Suit yourself," Haley calls after her, "but don't say I didn't warn you."

Destiny takes a detour on her way to her classroom and sees Curtis in the hallway. He's in a different homeroom than she is this year, so she has to go around the corner to find him.

I shouldn't be doing this, Destiny thinks. I shouldn't be letting Haley get to me like this. Curtis and I are fine – aren't we? I haven't seen him much in the last few weeks, but he would tell me if something was up between us. He would tell me if he wanted to break up with me. I know he would.

Curtis is standing in front of his locker like he's waiting for someone, so Destiny decides it would be a good time to talk to him and find out what's going on. Just before she reaches Curtis, Trinity comes bounding up to him. She takes his hand

and wraps his arm around her shoulder, tucking herself in close to him.

Destiny stops dead only a couple of feet in front of them. Trinity looks like she has won a great victory as she flashes a triumphant smile at Destiny. Curtis looks like he wants to be anywhere but there with the two of them.

"Curtis, I don't understand," Destiny says, working to keep her voice level. "What's going on?"

But it's Trinity who answers. "Come on, Destiny. Open your eyes. Can't you see?"

"See what," Destiny says, although she can see what's going on all too well. She just doesn't want to say it out loud because then it will seem so real, so final.

Trinity says it for her, through a wicked smile. "Curtis is going out with me now."

Destiny turns to Curtis. "Is it true?"

He nods. "I'm sorry," he says.

"You couldn't have the decency to tell me?" says Destiny in what is building into a rage.

"I meant to," says Curtis, "but you were always so busy and I never saw you and, well…" His face is beet red.

"How could you?" It's all Destiny can manage to say. She wants to maintain her dignity, so she turns and walks away from Curtis and Trinity.

She keeps on walking when she hears Curtis say her name, then she hears Trinity say, "Oh, let her go, Curtis. She's a big girl. She'll get over it."

Just keep walking, Destiny thinks to herself. Don't lose control here. Once the Destiny rounds the corner and is out of Curtis and Trinity's line of sight she runs to the bathroom in tears. There is no way she could ever get over it. It's the first time a boy has broken her heart.

Destiny is late getting to class, but she just didn't want anyone to see her crying. She hopes she doesn't have red eyes. As she walks to her desk, Haley smirks at her. Destiny does her best to ignore Haley as she takes her seat.

Destiny thinks back to the offer Mrs. Grant made at the end of last year. "You have a chance right now to advance to tenth grade, if you can prove that you are able to handle the subject matter. You would pass by the other students in your class and graduate high school a year early."

At the time she thought it would be best to stay in grade nine with the rest of her class, to stay with her friends, but maybe she made a mistake staying behind.

As the class gets ready to go to their first afternoon class, there is a knock at their homeroom door. Mrs. Pathway is there and Destiny gets a tight feeling in the pit of her stomach.

"Come on in, Mrs. Pathway," says Coach Strawberry.

"Thank you, Coach Strawberry," replies Mrs. Pathway, a stack of envelopes in her hand. "Class, I have the results of the ACT," she trills.

There is a lot of whispering as she passes out the results. As she hands Destiny her envelope, she says, "This is one of the best marks in the class, Destiny. Very impressive."

Destiny sits down and holds her envelope for a moment before opening it with shaking hands. Her score is 18.

Destiny can't help feeling disappointed. Even if it is one of the best scores in the class, she doesn't want the best in the class. She wants a high enough score not only to get into college, but to get a scholarship. It's the only way she will be able to go.

Mrs. Pathway addresses the class, "The scores were very impressive, especially since you are only in grade nine. You will take this practice test again in each of the next two years, and after that it will really count. Now that you know what to expect, you can do even better next year."

I will do better, thinks Destiny. I have to.

Destiny leans back in her seat. Forget Curtis and Trinity. Forget Haley. A big plan is forming in Destiny's mind. Yes, she has big things to do next year.

Part II:
Tenth Grade

Chapter 4
New Beginnings

T he grade ten year is coming to a close and the results for the year's ACT are in. Destiny rubs the back of her neck as she holds the envelope with her test score in her hands. Was missing her friends worth it?

The entire year has been such a blur. The Secret Sisters Club fell by the wayside and she has hardly seen Barbara and Julianna. It's probably a good thing that Curtis broke up with her last year because she wouldn't have had time for him anyway. On top of it all, she feels like all she's done for months is study.

That's probably because all I've done for months is study, thinks Destiny.

She opens the envelope and closes her eyes as she pulls out the results of her ACT. With a deep breath, she opens her eyes and looks.

Her score is 25.

Destiny feels like the whole thing is anticlimactic. After all the hard work she put in, she should have done better. Shouldn't she? Unsure of what her mark means for her future and unsure of where to go from here, Destiny packs up her books and gets ready for the bell to ring.

As she walks toward the door, merging with the flow of students leaving the classroom, Mrs. Grant calls out to her. "Destiny, can I have a word with you?"

A few classmates smile and nudge Destiny, joking around and saying, "Oh, you're in trouble."

Destiny gives them a frustrated look and walks over to Mrs. Grant's desk. "Yes, Mrs. Grant?"

"I wanted to know if you had made any decisions regarding your future," says Mrs. Grant.

"Do you mean my immediate future or more long-term?" asks Destiny.

"Both," replies Mrs. Grant with a smile.

"Well," says Destiny, now the only student left in the classroom, "I don't really know. I really wish I had skipped a grade last year when I had the chance. I did okay on my ACT, but I just don't know where to go from here."

"Destiny, your ACT score was better than okay." Destiny can hear the sincerity in Mrs. Grant's voice. "It was truly remarkable, especially for a student your age. You must understand that."

Destiny just nods her head, remaining unconvinced.

Mrs. Grant looks at Destiny for a long moment. "Destiny, if you were given another opportunity to skip a grade, would you take it?"

"Oh, yes," says Destiny. "I would jump at it. No one would be able to hold me back!"

"That is great, Destiny, because you have the opportunity to skip the 11th grade. Your hard work has paid off. Your grades and your score on the ACT have proven that you can handle the work, so if you are in agreement, I will see to the paperwork."

"Thank you, Mrs. Grant!" Destiny practically shouts she is so giddy with happiness and relief.

"You're welcome, dear," says Mrs. Grant, "Although, we really aren't giving you anything you haven't earned."

Destiny turns toward the door, ready to leave.

"Destiny," says Mrs. Grant. "Come and see me at lunchtime. You need to get to class right now and there is something else I want to discuss with you."

"Okay, Mrs. Grant," says Destiny, wondering what else Mrs. Grant could have to discuss with her. Destiny really doesn't want anything to ruin this moment, but a dark cloud hovers over her mood.

When the lunch bell rings, Destiny starts toward Mrs. Grant's classroom. Before she can get away, Barbara stops her and says, "Hey, Destiny. Do you want to have lunch together?"

"Sorry, Barbara," replies Destiny. "I have to go and see Mrs. Grant."

Barbara looks crestfallen. "I just thought, since the ACT is done and school is almost over, maybe we could hang out more often."

Destiny puts her hand on Barbara's shoulder, "Honey, I would love to. I really miss you and I promise we will hang out real soon, but right now I really have to run. Mrs. Grant is waiting for me."

"Okay, Destiny," Barbara says as she watches Destiny dart off down the hallway.

Destiny feels so guilty leaving Barbara just standing there, but she forgets her guilt and Barbara as soon as she walks into Mrs. Grant's classroom.

"Ah, Destiny, good. Bring a chair over here and have a seat," says Mrs. Grant from her desk.

Destiny does as she is told, and once seated, says, "What did you want to see me about, Mrs. Grant?"

"Well, Destiny," Mrs. Grant begins, "what do you have planned for this summer?"

"Nothing at this point," answers Destiny. "I was hoping to tutor and maybe help out as a teacher's assistant again."

"Well, there is a summer college program that I think would be very beneficial for you to attend."

"Really? You mean like actually going to college?" Destiny feels a bubble of excitement rising in her chest.

"Well, you wouldn't be enrolled in a college degree program," Mrs. Grant clarifies, "but it would give you an opportunity to earn some college credits that you can apply to your degree when you do go."

Destiny bounces up and down in her seat. "Where?" she asks.

"It's at Louisiana Tech, in Ruston. What do you think you would like to study?"

"Well," says Destiny, "I want to become a nurse."

"Perfect," says Mrs. Grant. "They have a summer medical program that you would be very interested in, I think."

"That would be so wonderful, Mrs. Grant!"

"Great. I will see to getting the paperwork to you so that you can get your application in." Mrs. Grant looks at Destiny with a very serious expression on her face. "You'll have to work hard, Destiny. Harder than ever before."

"Oh, I will," says Destiny. "Don't you worry about that, Mrs. Grant!"

"Fine, Destiny," says Mrs. Grant. "You run along now and have your lunch. And you'll need to talk this over with your folks, I'm sure, so you do that tonight and then we can take care of your application tomorrow."

Destiny face crumples into horror.

"What's wrong, Destiny?" asks Mrs. Grant.

"My parents," says Destiny in what is almost a whisper, "they can't afford to pay for a summer college program. I won't be able to go."

"Yes you will, Destiny," Mrs. Grant reassures her. "You will be going to this program on scholarship."

"Really?" asks Destiny, relief flooding through her. "My parents don't have to pay for anything?"

"Not a thing," says Mrs. Grant.

"Oh, thank you, Mrs. Grant!"

"Don't thank me, honey. You earned this with all your hard work. Now you run along to class, you hear?"

"Yes, maam!" Destiny leaves the classroom on cloud nine and wonders if she can find Barbara before lunch is over. It's a wonderful day to be alive!

Chapter 5
Bitter Sweet

When Destiny gets home after school, she finds her Momma in the kitchen starting dinner. She hasn't said anything to her friends about the summer program because she needs to talk to Momma first and make sure she can go. Destiny sincerely hopes she can go because it is the chance of a lifetime.

"Oh good, Destiny, honey," says Momma. "I'm glad you're home early today. You can start peeling those potatoes, please."

"Sure, Momma." Destiny picks up the knife and starts the rhythmic action of peeling. She always likes making dinner with Momma. It's nice to do something so mechanical. It lets her mind relax for a while.

"Did you have a good day, sugar?" asks Momma.

"Yes, Momma. Actually, I got some exciting news."

"Oh?"

Destiny stops peeling and takes a deep breath. "I spoke with Mrs. Grant today and she said I can go away for a summer college program."

"A summer college program?"

"Yes, Momma!" Once she starts talking about it, Destiny can't contain her excitement. "It's at Louisiana Tech and I can take a medical program and earn college credits for when I go to college for real."

"Okay, slow down, child," says Momma. "You're gonna give yourself a heart attack, or you're gonna give me one. Now you know your Pop and I ain't got no money to pay for your college and we ain't got no money to pay for this program, either."

"No, Momma, you don't have to pay for this. I can go on a scholarship."

Momma is silent for a moment. Finally, she says, "The whole cost is covered? We don't have to pay for anything?"

Destiny nods her head.

"Okay, child," says Momma. "You nod your head any faster and it will fly off your shoulders and then there goes any good sense you have."

"I can go?" asks Destiny, daring to hope.

"Yes, honey. I'm your Momma. I'm not gonna stand in your way. You go on and make us proud."

Destiny throws her arms around Momma. "Thank you so much, Momma. You will be proud of me. I'll show you, I promise."

"Oh, child, I know you will," says Momma, returning Destiny's hug. Then she straightens herself. "Now, college girl or not, those potatoes aren't gonna peel themselves."

"Yes, Momma." Destiny gets back to peeling the potatoes, thinking about how wonderful her summer will be.

The next morning on the bus, Destiny's mood is more sober because she realizes she has to break the news to Barbara that she won't be around for the summer. When Barbara gets on the bus, she makes her way back, plopping herself in the seat next to Destiny. Her purple dress looks radiant on her and her folded umbrella drips with the morning's drizzle as she drops it on the floor at her feet.

"Destiny, I'm so excited for this summer!" says Barbara. "My grandma is going to come here to visit us this summer, so I will be around the whole time. Plus, and this is the best part, Kendall will be coming to visit! It will be so good for the three of us to be able to hang out together again and without worrying about homework, studying, and stupid tests."

Oh boy, thinks Destiny. Telling Barbara she will be away this summer is going to be harder than she thought.

Barbara looks Destiny in the eye. "Okay, honey, I know that look. What have you got to tell me? You might as well spill the beans and get it over with."

"Well...," says Destiny.

"Let me guess. You are skipping grade 11."

"Actually, yes, but that's not all. You see, Barbara," Barbara already looks disappointed as Destiny starts to speak, "I'm the one who won't be here this summer."

"What do you mean? Where are you going?"

"I've been given the chance to go to a summer college program. I'll be in Ruston, Louisiana for the summer."

"Destiny," says Barbara, "That is so great. This is exactly what you've been wanting, to go to college." Destiny can hear the conflict in Barbara's voice, a conflict between utter disappointment and sincere happiness for her friend.

"Thanks, Barbara," Destiny replies. "I am really excited about it, but I am sorry we won't have the summer together. I would really like to hang out as much as we can before I go, okay?"

"Yeah, that'd be great," says Barbara, trying to sounds enthusiastic.

"Is Julianna staying around this summer?" Destiny asks.

"I think she will be away for some of it, but not all of it," answers Barbara.

"Well, at least you'll have her and Kendall to hang out with. I'm really sad that I'll miss Kendall's visit."

Barbara nods, "She will be sad to miss you, too."

As the bus pulls into the school, Destiny feels happy and sad at the same time. Things are changing so fast that she all of a sudden feels unsure of herself and her decision. Then she remembers her feeling of regret at not skipping grade nine when she had the chance. No, Destiny thinks, this is the right thing to do.

With that certainty firmly at the forefront of her mind, Destiny gets off the bus and walks into the school.

At lunchtime, Destiny meets with Mrs. Grant and fills out the application for the summer college program. "This is the beginning of an exciting future, Destiny," Mrs. Grant says. "You will do so many great things. I just know it."

"Thanks, Mrs. Grant," says Destiny. "Are you sure I'll get in?"

"Oh, yes, honey," Mrs. Grant assures her. "I have already spoken with admissions at Louisiana Tech. This paperwork is just a formality."

Destiny's excitement returns full force, her sadness at missing her friends forgotten, as she finishes filling out the application. "Thank you so much, Mrs. Grant. I can't wait."

"I bet you can't at that," replies Mrs. Grant. "And I can't wait to hear all about your adventures when you come back next year. I want you to come and tell me all about it as soon as you get back to school in September."

"I will," says Destiny.

"Wonderful. Have a good afternoon, Destiny."

"You, too, Mrs. Grant." Destiny walks out into the hallway and looks around her. Yup, things sure are changing fast, but they are definitely changing for the better.

Chapter 6
Summer Friendship

O*h, my*, thinks Destiny. *I don't know about this.* It is the first day of her summer classes and Destiny is both excited and terrified. She wonders if she belongs here at the college. Well, she's here now so she might just as well jump in with both feet and make a good impression.

Her first class is a wonderful class on clinical pathology. The teacher introduces himself, "Welcome to all of you. I am Professor Johnny Ray Blue. You are here because you are among the brightest of your peers and because you deserve to get a jumpstart on your future." Destiny wiggles with excitement. She hadn't really thought of it that way before.

Professor Blue goes on, "This is a clinical pathology class with a focus on carcinomas. Besides the lectures, you will also have a lab segment of the course, in which you will learn how to draw blood and create a realistic model of a part of the body of your choosing. By the time the course is finished, you will have a solid foundational knowledge in clinical pathology, including the flow of veins and arteries to and from the heart and brain."

With that, Professor Blue gives an introductory lecture and Destiny eagerly takes detailed notes. She finds it both fascinating and stimulating. It is all she can do to keep up with him, but she loves every moment of the class.

As Destiny is leaving the classroom after the lecture, she bumps into a boy who is walking down the hallway. "Oh, pardon me," says Destiny. "What a fool I am for not watching where I'm going."

The boy looks to be about Destiny's age. "Please, no," he replies. "It's my fault. My name is Alvin, Alvin Monsieur." He holds out his hand. "What's your name?"

"Destiny Sycamores," says Destiny, shaking Alvin's hand. "It's nice to meet you."

"Did you enjoy your class?" asks Alvin as they start walking down the hallway.

"Oh, yes, it was wonderful," says Destiny. "It's on clinical pathology and it is so fascinating. What are you taking while you're here?"

"I'm on a mission," replies Alvin. "I have come to America to become an engineer. So I am taking some introductory courses on civil and environmental engineering."

"Where are you from?" asks Destiny.

"Jamaica," Alvin answers. "Where are you from?"

"Nowhere nearly as exotic," says Destiny. "I'm from Many, Louisiana."

"It's exotic to me," says Alvin.

Destiny laughs and says, "I suppose it is."

When they walk out of the building, Destiny looks around hesitantly.

"Are you looking for something?" asks Alvin.

"I need to find the dorms. All my stuff was delivered there when I checked in this morning, but I haven't been there, yet. I'm just not sure where they are."

"I can show you," says Alvin. "I've got time before my next class."

"That's mighty kind of you, Alvin," says Destiny.

The two head off down the steps and turn left. "So, Destiny," says Alvin, "what do you do for fun?"

"Gee, I don't know," she replies. "I mean, I don't have a lot of time for extracurricular activities and stuff. I am pretty serious about my schoolwork. I do track though."

"Really?" Alvin sounds so excited, he can hardly contain it. "I do track as well!"

"What do you run?" asks Destiny.

"Various, but my specialty is the 400 and 800 hurdles. I'm coming here on a track scholarship next year."

"Wow, you must be fast."

"Yeah, I'm fast. I've won many races," says Alvin. "How about you?"

"I'm pretty fast, too, I guess. I'm a relay runner, 100, 200, 400, and 800. I've won some races with my team. My brother, Dino, though, he's the fast one in the family. He was the state champion in track, football, and basketball."

"Impressive!" says Alvin and stops walking. "Well, here's your dorm."

Destiny looks up to see a three-story red, brick building. "Thanks, Alvin. I hope I get to see you again."

"You can count on it," says Alvin. "See you around." And with that Alvin is gone.

Destiny walks down the hall on the second floor of the dorm, looking for her room number, 217. When she finds it, she puts her key into the lock and opens the door.

"Oh my goodness, you startled me," says a girl sitting on one of the beds.

"I'm sorry," says Destiny. "You must be my roommate and I think you were just in my clinical pathology class. Hi. My name's Destiny, Destiny Sycamores."

"Hi, Destiny," says the girl, holding out her hand. "I thought I recognized you. I'm Lynell Douglass."

"Really?" asks Destiny in surprise. "My first name is actually Linelle. How weird is that?"

"Too weird," says Lynell. "How do you spell your name?"

"L-I-N-E-L-L-E," says Destiny.

"I spell mine L-Y-N-E-L-L," says Lynell.

Destiny looks around the room. "I hope you don't mind I took this bed," says Lynell. "We can switch if you want."

"No, I'm fine with this bed," says Destiny, putting down her backpack on the bed on the right-hand side of the room and starting to unpack her suitcase. "Where are you from?"

"I'm from Sibley, Louisiana," says Lynell. "How about you?"

"I'm from Louisiana, too," says Destiny. "Many, Louisiana."

"Do you have any brothers or sisters?" asks Lynell.

"Yeah, I have two brothers and a sister. They're all older than me, though. You?"

"I have two older brothers, an older sister, and a younger sister who is blind."

"Wow," says Destiny, "that's a big family!"

"Yeah, I guess. I'm just so excited to be here though, partly get a break from them, but mostly because it's such an adventure!"

"Me, too," agrees Destiny.

AS the summer goes on, Destiny and Lynell become really good friends. Destiny spends time tutoring Lynell and some of the other students in her classes. Between that and her studies, she doesn't have time for much else.

One weekend, Lynell's family comes to town to visit and Destiny and Alvin are invited to dinner with the family. Destiny makes time for this dinner outing because she likes Lynell so much and wants to meet her family. Plus, she knows it's important to Lynell.

Destiny and Alvin meet Lynell and her family at the restaurant. When they get there, Lynell's family has already been seated and Destiny and Alvin are shown to the table. Lynell jumps up excitedly, "You guys made it. Come on. Everyone, this is Destiny – her first name is actually Linelle, like mine – and Alvin. Destiny and Alvin, these are my parents, Mr. and Mrs. Douglass, and my brother, Quentin."

"Hello, Destiny, Alvin," says Mrs. Douglass. "We have heard so much about you both."

"And, Destiny, I hear you are quite the tutor," says Mr. Douglass."

"She sure is, Pop," says Lynell. "She has helped me so much."

The dinner is buffet style and Destiny discovers Lynell is vegetarian. "I don't think I could ever be vegetarian," says Destiny to Lynell as she heaps loads of seafood onto her plate. Seafood is her favorite.

During dinner, while conversation is going around the table, Destiny feels Alvin's hand reach for hers under the table. She is sitting between Alvin and Lynell and once his hand finds hers, they hold hands for a while. It's the first time he has ever done anything like this and Destiny feels a warm flutter inside. But she doesn't have time for a boyfriend, does she?

Suddenly, Lynell taps Destiny on the shoulder. "I need to go to the ladies room. Destiny, come on!" Lynell practically pulls Destiny with her.

Once inside the washroom, Lynell turns and faces Destiny. "Okay, spill it. What's going on with you two?"

"Who two?" asks Destiny.

Lynell just gives Destiny a look that says, "Come on!"

"You caught the hand-holding, huh?" says Destiny.

"Um, yeah," replies Lynell. "Spill it!"

"I don't really know what's going on," says Destiny. "Honestly, I don't," she says after another look from Lynell. "Alvin just reached under the table and took my hand. He's never done anything like that before. I wasn't really sure he even liked me that way."

"Well, it's been pretty obvious to me," says Lynell. "So, what are you gonna do?"

"I don't know. I don't have time for a boyfriend, so I think I want to just stay friends."

"Honestly, Destiny, I knew you were gonna say that. I was hoping you weren't, but I knew you would."

When they got back to the table, Alvin was telling Lynell's family about how he wants to start his own engineering business one day. When dinner is over, everyone says goodbye and Lynell goes with her family to stay with them for the night in their hotel room. Destiny and Alvin walk back to campus.

"I hope you were okay with me holding your hand," says Alvin after they walked in silence for a while.

"Sure, I was," says Destiny.

"But...," says Alvin.

Destiny sighs. "But I have to focus on my studies. I just don't think now is the right time to get into a relationship. Besides, we don't even live in the same city."

"Well, not yet, anyway," says Alvin. "But I understand. My studies are important to me, too."

"Thank you," says Destiny, feeling relieved.

"Who knows," says Alvin. "Maybe we'll get a chance in a year or two, if you come here for college.

"Yeah, maybe," says Destiny, smiling and thinking about how lucky she is.

The next day, Destiny is helping Lynell with a project for one of their classes when the phone rings.

"I'll get it," says Lynell, reaching for the phone. Then she hands it to Destiny. "It's for you," she says.

Destiny takes the phone. "Hello." She nods her head. "Why would he do that, Momma?" Another pause. "Didn't he even think about us?" Pause. "Yes, okay. I love you, too. Goodbye." Destiny hangs up.

"What was that all about?" asks Lynell.

"My brother Dino just got married, but he didn't tell anyone. He just went and did it and we couldn't even be there."

"Oh, honey, I'm so sorry to hear that," says Lynell. "I'm sure he had his reasons."

"Yeah, but I don't know. Sometimes I wonder if my academic success is really worth all of this."

"All of what?" asks Lynell.

"The distance between me and my family and friends," says Destiny. "I just don't feel like I know them anymore."

"I get that, Destiny," says Lynell, "but you are following your heart, right?"

"I think I am," says Destiny.

"Well, honey, I sure hope so because I certainly can't tell you what path is right for you," says Lynell. "Only you can decide that for yourself."

Destiny nods her head in agreement. It's true that she has to choose her own path, but is this the right one? Deep in her heart, she truly doesn't know the answer to that question.

Chapter 7
Staying Focused

When Destiny gets back to school, she feels like a new person. She has made the decision to skip the eleventh grade, which means she will graduate this year. Her summer away was so amazing she can't imagine not going back there next year.

Destiny walks into her twelfth grade homeroom. As she looks for a seat, her gaze lands on Haley. For a moment, Destiny feels a twinge of frustration to see that Haley has been given the same opportunity as she has, to skip grade eleven, but then she thinks back to her summer and realizes that her competition with Haley doesn't matter anymore. Destiny has bigger and better things to strive for than besting Haley.

"Well, well, if it isn't Destiny Sycamores," says Haley. "They let you skip the eleventh grade? I guess there is just no accounting for today's standards."

Destiny keeps her mouth shut and finds an empty seat on the far side of the classroom. *Just keep thinking about going to college*, Destiny thinks. When she came into the school the previous week to sign up for grade twelve, Mrs. Grant said to her, "You have to get your mind right, child. This is going to be a big year for you." Getting her mind right is exactly what Destiny plans to do and that starts with ignoring Haley.

At lunch, Barbara finds Destiny at her locker. "So this is where all you cool twelfth graders hang out," she says as Destiny closes her locker.

"Hi, Barbara!" says Destiny, giving her friend a hug.

"Oh, Destiny, I really have missed you," says Barbara.

"Me, too." Destiny only got back from Louisiana Tech last week, so she hasn't had time to get together with Barbara. This is the first time she's seen her.

"So," says Barbara, "can we hang out after school today? You know, before homework sucks you in and I don't see you for the rest of the year?"

"Awe, Barbara, I'd love to, but I have to go to work today."

"That's perfect," says Barbara. "I need to work on math, so we can work together and you can tell me all about your summer. I'm dying to hear about it."

The guilt creeps in as Destiny says, "Actually, Barbara, I mean I have to go to work. I got a job at the grocery store and I start today after school."

"A job? How on earth have you had time to find a job? You just got back."

"My Pop set it up for me. I'm saving up to buy a car and I don't have much more to go before I have enough money."

"Oh, okay," says Barbara, trying to keep the disappointment out of her voice. "Well, when will you have a chance to help me with my math?"

"I have a tutoring session next week, so I can help you then."

"Next week!" shouts Barbara. "But I have a big test coming up on Friday and I was really hoping you could help me."

Destiny feels bad. "I'm sorry, Barbara. Really I am. I'm just so busy this week. If I can find any free time before Friday, I'll let you know."

"Yeah, sure," says Barbara. "Don't worry about it. I'll figure it out." Destiny watches Barbara turn and walk away. She feels that there is nothing she can do but watch Barbara go.

Working at the grocery store seems easy enough, thinks Destiny. For the first two hours of her shift, a woman showed her how to use the cash register to ring people through. Now Destiny is on her own while her trainer is on her break. But when the next customer comes through, something goes wrong and she can't figure out what.

Just then a boy walks by. He's wearing a store uniform, so Destiny says, "Excuse me. Can you help me with the register? There's something wrong."

"Sure. You're new here aren't ya. What's your name?"

"Destiny. What's Yours?"

"I'm Drake. Let's see what the problem is here."

Destiny turns to her customer. "It'll just be a moment, mam." The woman nods and Destiny turns back to Drake and the cash register.

Drake stops fiddling with the register and looks at Destiny. "Now wait just a darn minute. What do I get for helping you with this register?"

"Um... I...," Destiny doesn't know what to say.

"How about in exchange for me helping you," Drake says, "you go out on a date with me."

Destiny didn't know what to say. Her customer was waiting and the register had to be fixed. "Well, I... I'm sure I can figure it out, thanks."

Drake lets out a big laugh. "It's okay. I'm just pulling your leg. Here, you just need to push this button."

"Oh, okay, thanks," says Destiny.

"But I would like to go out with you sometime."

"Ok, well, maybe someday," replies Destiny.

That night at home the phone rings. "It's for you, Destiny," shouts Momma. "He says his name is Drake."

Destiny takes the phone and talks to Drake for a long time. When she finally hangs up, her Momma says, "Now what were you doin' talkin' so late on the phone with that boy."

"Oh, we were just talking about work, Momma," says Destiny.

"Uh huh," says Momma, "Sure child, sure."

That night, Destiny has a dream about her Grandma Lucy-Belle. She and Grandma are sitting on the couch in Destiny's living room and Grandma Lucy-Belle says, "Child, now don't you go foolin' around, you hear? You stay focused on your books and get yourself a good education."

"I know grandma," says Destiny. "It wouldn't hurt to have a date with Drake, though, would it?"

"Now you think about that, child," says Grandma. "You chose not to get together with that nice boy Alvin. Why did you choose that?"

Destiny sighs. "Because I need to focus on my studies," she says. "But, can I really change anything. Can I make a difference in my life, in the world?"

Grandma Lucy-Belle looks Destiny in the eye and says, "Now you listen here. You stay focused on your books because your books will help you. They won't lie to you or cheat on you and that's knowledge that nobody can take away from you. Listen to me, Linelle Destiny. You have a chance to move our family forward and start a healthy family blueprint that will last for many years to come."

"Yes, Grandma," Destiny says.

Destiny wakes up, Grandma Lucy-Belle's voice still echoing in her mind. Stay focused on your books. Destiny has a strange feeling she should listen.

The next day after school, Destiny is tutoring some students in the library when flowers are delivered. The librarian points to Destiny and the courier brings the flowers to her.

"Hear you go, miss," he says.

"Uh, thank you," Destiny says. "Who are they from?"

"There's a card." And with that the courier is gone.

Destiny looks at the card that came with the flowers. It says: *I saw these flowers and they reminded me of you. Drake*

Barbara looks at Destiny and raises her eyebrow. "You have a boyfriend and you haven't told me?" she says accusingly.

"He's not my boyfriend," says Destiny. "He's just a guy I work with at the grocery store. He's asked me out on a date a few times, but I always turn him down."

"You could always take him as your date to the prom," says Julianna.

"If I go to the prom," says Destiny. "I might go to senior skip day instead. Really, I honestly don't know what I'll do."

Barbara raises her eyebrow again, "Destiny Sycamores, if only I had your problems."

"Let's just get back to our lesson," says Destiny. She doesn't want to think about it right now because the decision is just too hard to make.

Chapter 8

The Car, the Boy, and the Future

T he day has finally arrived! Destiny can hardly contain herself as Momma pulls into the used car lot. She can't ever remember being this excited about anything, not ever! Not even Christmas morning or going to Louisiana Tech last summer. *Ok, maybe Louisiana Tech was as exciting*, thinks Destiny.

Momma parks and they get out of the car. "Show me the car you want, sugar," says Momma.

"It's over there, Momma," says Destiny, pointing across the lot. They walk over.

"My, you almost need a car to get to your car," says Momma. "This lot is big."

"It is," replies Destiny, wishing she could just run over to the car, pay, and drive away. Of course, she remembers her manners and stays with Momma.

"There are a lot of nice cars here, Destiny," Momma says as they reach Destiny's car. "Which one is yours?"

"This one," says Destiny, gesturing to a money-green 1997 Ford Contour.

Destiny's Momma looks the car over. "Now, honey, you're sure this is the one you want? It looks a little shabby. There are a lot of others that might be a little newer and a little cleaner lookin'."

"Oh, no, Momma," says Destiny. "I'm absolutely positive. This is the car I want." She had probably walked past the car lot at least once a week for months, waiting for the right car to appear. When she saw this one last month, she knew it was the one for her.

"Can I help y'all," says a voice from behind Destiny and Momma.

"Mercy, but you gave me a start," says Momma, turning around.

"Sorry, mam. I do apologize."

"That's quite alright. My daughter is here to buy a car."

The man looks at Destiny, "Well, you have come to the right place. My name is Mr. Robinson and I am happy to help. You have a car in mind?"

"Yes, sir. My name is Destiny and I would very much like to buy this car, right here." Again, Destiny gestures to the Ford.

"That's a fine choice, miss," says Mr. Robinson. "Let's go inside and do up the paperwork.

"Now, hold on," says Momma. "I want to make sure you ain't sellin' my baby a lemon, no disrespect intended, sir."

"None taken, mam. I understand perfectly. This car works just fine. We gave it a good tune up when it arrived last month and we offer a full one-year warranty on all parts."

Momma nods her approval and we go into the dealership to fill out the paperwork. Once everything is signed, Destiny pulls out her money, everything she has saved from tutoring and her job at the grocery store. It feels like so much money when she hands it to Mr. Robinson. He then excuses himself and disappears for a short while.

"Destiny, honey," says Momma, "stop all that fidgetin'."

"Sorry, Momma."

Mr. Robinson returns. "Well, Miss Destiny," he says, holding out a set of keys. "You are the proud new owner of a 1997 Ford Contour."

Destiny takes the keys and says, "Thank you so much!"

"Now, there is a temporary licence plate on the car for now, until you receive your personalized plate in the mail."

Destiny had ordered a personalized Tweety Bird license plate that says "SHORTY" on it. "Just to make it unique and totally mine," Destiny said when Momma had given her a questioning look.

"It's your money, I suppose," Momma had said.

They walk back out to the car and Destiny unlocks the door and gets in.

"Now, it has a full tank of gas," says Mr. Robinson. "But don't go using that all up today now, ya hear?"

"No sir, I won't," says Destiny. Then she looks at Momma. "Can I go now, Momma? I want to drive by work and show Drake my new car."

Momma gives Destiny a long look and then smiles. "Yes, girl. You run along now, but be home in time for dinner."

"Yes, Momma. I will!" With that, Destiny starts the car and drives out of the lot, feeling like she's on top of the world.

Destiny parks her car in the grocery store parking lot and goes to find Drake. She doesn't have to go far. She walks around the corner to go into the store and Drake is near the door. But he's not alone. He's kissing a girl, one Destiny has never seen before. She stops dead, feeling the same way she did when she found out Curtis was going out with Trinity.

Destiny turns around and runs back to her car, but she hears footsteps behind her. She opens the door and Drake is there, right behind her.

"Destiny, wait!" he says. "Really, there's nothing with that girl."

"Oh, really," says Destiny, getting into her car.

She goes to shut the door, but Drake grabs it and holds it open. "Really, Destiny. She's just a girl I know. We've hung out a few times, but I'm into you, honey."

"Well, I'm not into you anymore, Drake," says Destiny. "Please, let go of my door."

Drake let's go and Destiny closes the door, starts the car, and drives away. When she gets home, she pulls into the drive-way behind Momma's car and goes into the house. She runs to the living room, throws herself onto the couch, and cries herself to sleep.

When Destiny wakes up, the house is quiet and she doesn't know what time it is. She sits up and then she is somewhere else. She is sitting in the back yard with her Grandma Lucy-Belle. It's late afternoon and the sun is starting to get low in the sky.

"Grandma, I don't understand," says Destiny. "Why does this keep happening to me? Why don't boys like me?"

"Oh, child," replies Grandma. "These ain't the boys that matter. And besides, you need to focus on your books. They're what you need right now."

"I know, but does that mean I can't have a boyfriend, too?"

Grandma Lucy-Belle looks Destiny straight in the eye. "It means things will happen when the time is right and not before."

The next thing Destiny knows, she can see herself. She's older, but not too much. She is in Paris, then she's in London. She sees herself in different cities around the world, standing in front of groups of people, talking to them and sharing her knowledge with them. Then Grandma Lucy-Belle is in front of her once again.

"What was that?" Destiny asks.

"That was your future, child."

"Is that really what life has in store for me," asks Destiny. "You can show me that?"

"Yes, honey," answers Grandma. "But only if you stick to your books. You'll find a boy, too, one day. When the time is right, you will find a boy that'll treat you right. Don't you worry about that, now, ya hear?"

Destiny nods.

"It's all up to you, child," says Grandma. "You make your future and if you want that future, you gotta make the right choices."

Grandma Lucy-Belle fades away and Destiny finds herself still sitting on the couch. She feels at peace. Then she hears Momma come in the back door. "Destiny, come help get dinner ready."

"Okay, Momma," calls Destiny. As she goes to the kitchen, Destiny knows what she needs to do. Her Grandma Lucy-Belle has shown her.

Chapter 9
Senior Skip Day

Destiny is closing her locker when Barbara and Julianna come up to her.

"Hey, Destiny," says Julianna.

"Hi guys," says Destiny.

"Barbara and I thought we'd catch up with you and chat before class starts," says Julianna.

Barbara nods. "We wanted to know if you wanted to hang out at lunch. Kind of like the old days, you know?"

"I'd love to," says Destiny, "but today is senior skip day. I'm going to that."

"Oh, right," says Barbara. "I see."

"Listen, I'm really sorry, but it's a big deal, especially since I'm not going to the prom," says Destiny. She had to choose one or the other, and with no date, going to the prom didn't make much sense.

"We know, Destiny," says Julianna. "It's just that we want to spend some time with you before you graduate."

58

"You're leaving us behind," says Barbara flatly. "It feels like you're already gone and you haven't even graduated and left the school, yet."

Destiny doesn't know what to say. Barbara sounds almost angry. "I'm not leaving you behind," says Destiny. "I'm graduating early, but I'm not going away. I'll still be living at home and we can hang out."

Barbara gives her that look she has, the one with raised eyebrows. "Come on, Destiny. You barely have time for us when we go to the same school and you have a high school work load. How can you possibly believe we will ever see you once you go to college?"

"You will," says Destiny. "I'll find a way."

Barbara just rolls her eyes, but Julianna says, "I know you mean that, Destiny, I really do. It's just that once you get there, to college I mean, it will be a whole new world."

Destiny looks at her two friends, feeling a big rift forming between them. "I'm not going to forget about you guys, you know. I wish you could just be happy for me."

"We are happy for you, Destiny," says Julianna. "We just miss you, that's all. Will you have lunch with us?"

Destiny hesitates. Should she spend the time with her friends instead of going to senior skip day?

Just then Kevin, another senior, comes running up. "Come on, Destiny." He sounds out of breath. "A bunch of us are heading out to get things started. We need your help setting up. You have all the notes." Destiny is the Senior Class Secretary, so she took the notes at the senior skip day planning meeting.

Destiny looks at her friends.

Barbara says, "Just go."

Julianna says, "Goodbye, Destiny."

Destiny has a feeling Julianna's goodbye is final, like she won't see them again. Kevin says, "Come on!" He grabs Destiny's arm and pulls her down the hall. Destiny follows, an empty feeling in the pit of her stomach.

"I think we're all set up," says Kevin as the senior class gathers around. There are different stations where they can play cards, play musical chairs, throw water balloons, and do other fun activities. Everyone disperses to their chosen activities. The sun is shining, the day is warm, and soon Destiny forgets her feelings of sadness and disappointment in Barbara's and Julianna's reaction to her graduating early.

Lunch consists of a barbecue and other delicious snacks. Around mid-afternoon, Mike Mitchell comes up to Destiny and says, "Destiny, what about one more race for old time's sake?"

"Do you really want to get beat one last time, Mike?" says Destiny. She and Mike had raced many times over the years and Destiny had always won.

"No," says Mike. "I want to go out with a bang by beating you this time."

"Uh huh," says Destiny, but she lets Mike win the race because she wants to give him that gift and keep the memory of their races alive.

They wind down the afternoon with a pep rally and a senior meeting to prepare for graduation. Destiny can feel the school spirit sizzling through the senior class as they finish the meeting and start cleaning up from senior skip day. Everyone had fun and they are all excited for graduation.

It is late when Destiny gets home and Momma has her dinner set aside. "How did your skip day go?" Momma asks as Destiny eats.

"It was really fun, Momma. We had lots of great activities and food."

"That's good, child," says Momma. "You hold on to those fun times, now, you hear? You gonna be working hard in college and life is busy. Have fun while you can."

"Yes, Momma," replies Destiny.

After she helps clean up from dinner, Destiny goes to her room and lies down on her bed. She puts her hands behind her head and thinks about life. She is about to graduate from high school go to college and wonders if she really is ready.

Destiny thinks about the last few years. It has been crazy, but she has worked really hard to get to where she is now. She deserves this chance and Destiny decides that if she isn't ready now, then she never will be.

"I'm ready to graduate," Destiny says to herself. "College, here I come!"

Epilogue

Graduation day is later in the week and Destiny is thrilled. She's not only excited about graduating, but she is hoping she is chosen as valedictorian. The classes are heading to the final assembly of the year, and as they line up outside the gym door, Destiny shifts her weight back and forth from one foot to the other. She knows if Momma were here right now she would tell Destiny to stop fidgeting.

"Destiny, calm down," says Barbara. "That fidgeting won't get us in the gym any faster."

Destiny tries to stay still, but it's hard. Finally, they go into the gym and take their seats. Mr. Gabriel gets up in front of everyone and says, "Welcome everyone. It's hard to believe another year is almost done. I'm proud of all of you for the effort you have put forth." Everyone applauds.

Mr. Gabriel looks around the gym. "I'm especially proud of our graduating class," he continues. "I know you have all worked hard and that hard work will pay off. I would like to congratulate one person in particular. She has proven herself again and again with hard work and perseverance and I am happy to announce she will be this year's valedictorian. Please give a warm round of applause to Haley Davis."

The applause thunders through the gym, and as Haley stands in triumph, she winks at Destiny. Destiny slumps in her seat. How could Haley have been chosen as valedictorian? Of course, Destiny knows the answer to that question. She feels bad for being upset, but she can't help remembering that Haley spent the whole year filing her nails in class and cheating on tests. It's just not fair.

Graduation day arrives and Destiny's insides feel as though they are in a tizzy. Graduating a year early, leaving high school behind, going off to college, and being beat out for valedictorian by Haley have created a chaotic mix of emotions in her.

When the graduating class goes into the gym in their caps and gowns, they walk up the center aisle between the rows of parents and families and take their seats in the front few rows that are reserved for them. Destiny sits on her hands to keep from fidgeting.

Mrs. Sparks approaches the podium. "Welcome everyone!" she says and waits for the crowd to quiet down. When it's quiet, Mrs. Sparks says, "I would like to ask Destiny Sycamores to come up and lead us in the Pledge of Allegiance.

Destiny is stunned and nervousness sets in immediately. Somehow, she gets up and walks to the podium. As she stands there looking out over the crowd, all of the practice speaking in front of others she had in the eighth grade fly out of her head.

"I pledge allegiance to the f-f-flag," she stutters. Everyone laughs as they join in. Destiny is devastated, but she keeps going, finishing the Pledge and thinking she'd just mess up a valedictorian speech anyway. Still, she wishes she had the chance to tell everyone she's proud of them.

When the Pledge is done, Mrs. Sparks nods to Destiny and Destiny takes her seat. She can feel her face is beet red. "Thank you Destiny," says Mrs. Sparks. "Now I will ask everyone to please welcome the valedictorian of the 2001 graduating class of Skyline High School, Haley Davis."

A round of applause erupts as Haley stands and makes her way to the podium. She delivers her speech, but Destiny barely hears it because she's caught between the embarrassment from her own stuttering a moment ago and her anger at Haley.

When Haley is finished her speech, she steps down, giving Destiny a smug look. With that look Destiny practically smoulders in her seat. She hates that Haley has the satisfaction of rubbing this in her face.

Once Haley is seated again, Mr. Gabriel comes to the podium. "Welcome, graduating class of 2001," says Mr. Gabriel. He goes on to say what is only supposed to be a few words, but seems to take forever. Then they call the graduates up one at a time.

"Linelle Destiny Sycamores," calls Mr. Gabriel, finally.

This is it, thinks Destiny, and all thoughts of Haley disappear as she walks up and proudly accepts her high school diploma. Smiling she looks out to her family and she can see Momma is crying.

I did it, thinks Destiny. *Now I will go to college and I won't have to put up with Haley anymore.* The day couldn't be more perfect. Destiny enjoys the rest of the ceremony as she clasps her diploma tightly.

On the way home, Destiny's mother says, "Destiny, child, why did you stutter when you were saying the Pledge of Allegiance?"

"Oh, Momma," Destiny says, feeling embarrassed all over again and grateful that it is only Momma and Pop in the car, "I was nervous, that's all."

Destiny knows she hasn't been working on speaking in front of others and feels bad about it, but schoolwork got in the way. Plus, she hasn't had to stand up and talk in front of the class since the poem she had to recite in eighth grade.

"Well now, child, what are you talking about?" says Momma. "I know I've never heard you stutter at home."

Destiny shrugs and says, "Well, Momma, I guess I never get nervous at home."

"You gonna have to get over that, honey. Ain't no way you gonna make it in the world, especially teaching people, if you gonna stutter like that every time you speak to 'em."

"Yes, Momma," says Destiny. She can see her Pop nodding in agreement and she knows Momma is right. She is going to have to get better at speaking in front of people. After all, she's off to college this summer, and like Momma said, there is no way to avoid speaking in front of people if she's going to be a teacher.

About the Author

Alicia Linelle Holland was born and raised in Many, Louisiana and got her middle name after her mother, Vera Linelle. When Alicia was in middle school, she started the Secret Sister Club that you read about in the Linelle Destiny Book Series. Alicia Holland has been working towards bringing back the Secret Sister Club as she embarks upon quite an interesting life and spiritual journey. At age 26, she earned her Doctorate in Education so that she can be in a position to help others believe in themselves and go far. At age 31, Dr. Alicia Holland opened a Not for Profit, Alise Spiritual Healing & Wellness Center and was officially ordained as a Minister. As a Transformational Life Coach, Professor, Author, Speaker, and Minister, Dr. Holland travels the World sharing her message: "You are Loved, You are Valued, and You are Competent.

Dr. Alicia Holland has two beautiful daughters, ages 7 and 9, who travels the World with her and are active participants in the Secret Sister Club Mentoring Program. She and her family resides in Austin, Texas and are currently looking for a new puppy.

Dr. Holland is available for speaking engagements and can be reached at support@thesecretsistersclub.com or support@iglobaleducation.com.

www.ingramcontent.com/pod-product-compliance
Lightning Source LLC
Chambersburg PA
CBHW071205130626
46555CB00004B/1590